Parents and children alike will appreciate reliving the escapades of Lewis and Clark, as author David L. Miller brings to life adventures from the early 1800's, on the pages of <u>A Travelerz Trew Tale</u>. This read is not only educational and well illustrated, but also fun and entertaining. A read the entire family will enjoy discovering!

~ Peg Yoder,
Homeschool Mom of six adventurous children

I thoroughly enjoyed reading "A Travelerz Trew Tale." It's a breath of fresh air. David did his research well, and the result is more than a fictionalized historical novel. It's an historically accurate description of Lewis and Clark's famous expedition, as told in the words of an imaginary fur trapper, Daniel Mueller, who joins the group soon after it starts out. His first-hand description of the explorers' many struggles and their ultimate success makes learning history as fun as reading a good book. I'll be looking forward to seeing David's next project!

~ Roland Stuckey, M.D.

A TRAVELERZ TREW TALE

~ ~ ~ ~ ~ ~

MY JOURNEY WITH LEWIS & CLARK

DANIEL MUELLER

SEPTEMBER, 1837

© 2015 ~ David Lynn Miller, Author
© 2015 ~ Stacy Lynn Andrews, Sketch Artist
© Common Domain ~ Lewis & Clark, illustrations
© 2005 ~ {map} ~ compliments of www.franksrealm.com

© 2016 David Lynn Miller

All Rights Reserved.

No part of this publication may be reproduced, stored in a retrieval system, or transmitted, in any form or by any means, electronic, mechanical, photocopying, recording, or otherwise, without the written permission of the author.

First published by Dog Ear Publishing
4011 Vincennes Rd
Indianapolis, IN 46268
www.dogearpublishing.net

ISBN: 978-1-4575-4527-6

This book is printed on acid-free paper.

This is a work of Historical Fiction. Only the main character is fictitious. All other information included, excepting that of said main character, is historically accurate. Any errors are soley the responsibility of the author.

Printed in the United States of America

This work is dedicated to

Mrs. Dorothy Hutchins

without whose encouragement

it might never have been completed.

{ Proverbs 3:5-6 }

{One of the oldest members of our northwest Ohio community, Mrs. Rebekah Lynne (Mueller) Hutchinstotter, passed away recently. Buried deep in an old cedar chest, her great-grandchildren discovered the following. It was scribbled in faded, scratchy handwriting on what appeared to be quite antique parchment. From the date indicated, it is estimated that this Journal goes back approximately seven generations.

All indications are that the work is authentic.}

THESE OLD BONES don't werk near as good as they used to back in the days wen I went a solderin with Captans Lewis an Clark an the Core of Discuvery. My wife Emma an I have been mighty blessed of God to live these 30 sum yeers here in northwest Ohia. We raised a family of four younguns, now fully grown. I'm in my 50's these days.

Not long ago we found the Jernal I wrote back wen I was on my own an explorin with the Expudishun. I read that ole Jernal again, an sketched in sum pictures so ya'll kin see a bit of wut I saw. I even tried on my old clothes. It gave me a chuckle cause they don't fit neer as good as they did back in the day. I hope my experiences make fer interestin readin, an you kin feel like you are seein an doin the things I saw an did back wen I wuz young.

A TRAVELERZ TREW TALE

My Journey with Lewis & Clark

~ FURST PART ~

Howdy. Let me start off by introdusin myself. My name's Daniel Mueller, but most folks call me Danny. I'm a hunter an traper by trade, livin up in the Northwest Teritoree. Wen I wuz about 22 yeers old, I come ta travel with Captans Lewis and Clark on wut they call their Core of Discuvery. I no I can't read or rite too good, but wut I knowz I think should be rote down for others to know about too. Most of the other fellas in the Core is writin about by the Captans, but fer sum rezon it looks like they plum fergot about me. I no I don't do all that much in the line of explorin or bein brave or stuff like that, but it aint as tho I don't exist. Taint fair, that's wut I say, so heres my piece of the story.

TA START OFF WITH, I was born in the old Kentukee lands, wut wuz then part of Virginny, in the year of 1782. It wuz a reel wild country back in them days, but people wuz startin ta moov into the region more an more all the time. There weren't naybors fer many a mile, an fer the most part we liked it jest fine that way. My fokes came ta Kentukee ta git away from a huge pile a back bills they wuz owin, an ta look fer sum new, rich soil ta farm. Land wuz reel cheep in them days, an all it took wuz a handshake ta buy the land, sinse a man's word wuz neerly as good as cash. They'd pay fer it a bit at a time when the crops came in each yeer. Most of the area is cuvered with trees, so a lot of farmin had to do with clearin the land afer ya cood grow stuff on it. As I grew up, yungins my age went ta skool durin the months wen the plantin or harvestin weren't bein dun, but as soon as the season kicked in, skool let out fer us. That's how I got myself a little bit of edjucashun. I spoze most city fokes get better skoolin, but fer us on the fronteer, us boys had ta do are chores and the girls learned ta keep house, so skoolin just came fer us wherever it fit in.

    I lerned reel quick that I dint care fer farmin much, so as soon as I cood I joined up with sum hunters an trapers ta lern the trade. They showed me how the werk wuz dun, an they told me I latched on reel quick. Any dang fool kin go out tryin ta hunt or fish or trap. All they need is a lot of luck. But to be mitey fine at any of them things, ya gotta take the senses the good Lord giv ya an put em together with the skills ya lern over time, an do things right. God give ya a noze ta sniff with, eyes ta see with, ears ta lissen proper with, an inner senses ta feel things out with that jest can't be described in werds. Ya gotta lern ta think like a fish, like a bird, like a critter. Wen ya know how they'd act an where they'd hide, then ya kin catch em. My huntin frends lerned me all of that an more besides.

　　Wen I was about 18, it occurred ta me that we wuz gettin trapped~out in the area where I wuz, so I set out north an west, lookin fer untouched land. In time, I came ta the teritorees called Indiana an Ilinoys ~ part of the Northwest Territory rejun. Critters wuz abununtly plentiful, an it wuz like I wuz in heaven! I could catch all I wanted fer tradin, an find all the meet I could shoot fer their hides ta sell or trade an ta keep

A Travelerz Trew Tale

me in food til I wuz full ta burstin. There wuz squirels an rabits an coons an bufalo an deer an bear an elk all over the place. I wooda ben a fool not ta take this place fer a home, wich is wut I dun. A fella cood go fer munths without seein another human, an that wuz fine with me. It kinda reminded me of my growin up yeers wen Kentukee wernt so full o folks. I carried around with me a cuple of old letters from my family back in Kentukee, jest ta remind me of thoz old dayz. I got em out frum time ta time an read em ta remind me wut wuz said.

I got used ta bein alone, fer the most part. I even preferred being out in the quiet, with only me an God and the criters. There wuz plenty of Injuns ta watch out fer, them not likin us wites livin in there huntin lands, an I cood understand that. But I steerd clear of em fer the most part, jest the same. Most tribes in those parts is sorta tame an kin be trusted, but sum of em wus reel killers an them wus ta be avoided at all costs. There is also animuls like wolves an bares an cyotees an snakes ta keep an eye out fer, but in general, a careful fella is a safe fella.

Its perdy hard ta travel very far wen you have to carry everthin all by yerself. I had my traps, my rifle, gunpowder, bullets, a lead stick ta melt down so as ta make more bullets, a nife fer skinnin, an a coat an vest an britches all made of buckskin ta keep the rain off. Sumtimez I wore a hat ta keep the sun outta my eyes and the rain offa my face, but other timez, like when it was cold, I kep a coon-skin cap handy fer the warmth. Naturally I had ta carry extra food with me, like baked corn or wheat biskuts, hardtack, and dried beef, venisun, and any other meets. Then too therez the pelts frum the animuls ya skinned. It turnd out ta be a heavy load, but I got used to it reel soon cause I had ta.

~ SECUND PART ~
WESTWARD TRAVAIL

Wen I first come across the men of the Lewis an Clark expudishun, I wuz trapin, a fer peece West of the Ohia country, on a crick off the Mizura River, where the beever, mink and coon were thick as flies. I herd these fellers down on the river, caterwalin an carryin on somthin fierce, disturbin my peese an scarin off the criters. I wuz so mad I cooda cussed about them makin all that rakit. But I knew from experiense that I'd better check em out an see wut they wuz about afer I stuck my neck out an let em know I wuz there. Qwik as I cood I snuk over ta see wut all the fuss wuz about.

Bein able ta sneak quiet~like thru the underbrush an leafs an twigs that might be hidden underfoot is another speshul tool of the hunter, an I wuz good at it.

So there wuz all them fellas rowin hard, werkin their way upstreem with a mighty effert agin the current. A lot of em wuz polin one big keelbote ~ that's a bote with a flat bottom, a cabin on the stern, an most of the deck cleer, so men kin row or pole it along ~ that wuz loded down with everthin you cood imajun. Other men were on the shore, lookin at the plants an critters an rocks an bugs like they'd just discoverd gold or sumthin. I'd seen it all afer ~ jest common wildlife as far as I cood tell. But they seemed ta think it was all new an speshul sumhowz. As they traveled up the Mizura that day, I slunk along the far shore soze they couldn't see me but soze I could see wut all the dang comotion wuz about. Dusk wuz comin on, so they anchored the big keelbote in mid river, ta protect em frum Injuns, just lik I'd do myself.

I krept up closer an heered em speakin English of all things! I guessed they might be Amerikuns, jest like me, so I come in close. After quite a spell I stepped out into the open along the shore an introdused myself...sorta made myself unhid. One of the men come up ta me an asked me wut I wanted. I tole him I wuz curious about them'uns, so he took me over ta meet a fella with blazin red hair.

"Captan William Clark is my name," he said as he introdused hisself," an that man over there," he said, pointing, "is the leader of are group, Captan Merrywether Lewis."

Followin sum questionin to find out what I wuz up to, he musta decided I was ok. He invited me to join em at the campfire for some vittles, an then went on ta explain," I, along with all of the other men in this venture for the American goverment are explorin the vast lands west of the Misisipi River, which we just bought from the French. We hope to find a waterway leedin up the Mizura an all the way to the Pasific, if there be one. Along the way, we are also ta greet as many Injun tribes as we kin an make frends with em if possible. We are charged by Prezident Jefersun to collect plant and animul samples, as well as map out our progress westward, returning as promptly as we kin."

I told him wut all I could do, like hunt an fish an trap reel good. Since I knew the land hereabouts, an most a them dint, they wuz interested in findin out wut I knew about the area. I wuz reely interested in their plans, hopin mebbe I could go along, but I dint want ta say so right off.

Captan Clark then told me that one of their men had died not long afer ~ Sarjunt Floid, he told me his name wuz ~ so he figgered they cood use an extra hand. He sed Floid had a horibl gut ache fer quite a wile, an even Dr. Rush's "Thundrboltz" coodn't cure him. I asked wut them "Thundrboltz" wuz, an Captan Clark explained. "A lot of the time, wen a body gits sick, its got diferent kinds of poisons in the blood.

Many docters bleed their patients ta help em git better. But Dr. Rush, a medicine man over in Philadelfia, had trained Captan Lewis to use these pills to purge the poisons out of the body. Yer guts get cleaned out, that's fer sure," he added with a wink. The men thot Floid had the Colik, an it wuz probly already set in afer he joint the Expudishun. But personally, I had seen fellas who had teribl gut akes like that an it turned out there upendix had exploded; mebbe that's wut happened ta Sarjunt Floid, who knows?

    Anyhow, after they decided ta ask me ta join em, I wuz sworn in as a Pryvit, this bein a completely militaree expudishun, ta surv as a scout and huntr. They issued me a sword as a regular army man, an I ware it proudly. That's where I officially signed into the Core of Discuvery ~ jest a bit upriver frum Floyd's Bluff, neer where he wuz buried, on a hill beside the Mizura River.

It wuz then that Captan Lewis took me aside, put his arm around my shoulders an put his head close ta mine, speakin softly, "Danny, this is a military venshur an we need ta treat it as such. Since we jest bought this Lueeziana Territory, there are French, British, an Spanish who either don't yet know about the Purchase or if they do, they may be agin it, so we are goin into wut cood be considered enemy lands. They may try ta stop us, or even harm us. We need ta be careful an not tell all we know to whoever we meet. If we come across strangers, Captan Clark an I will do the talkin, until we know who weer dealin with. Is that cleer?"

"Yessir," I sed. "I understand."

"Very good," he sed. "Now, go meet the rest of the Core ~

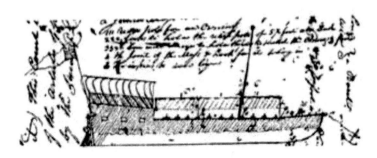

[Key to Drawing]

a Jointed Mast to let down of 32 feet long
1 1 1 Ridge poles for an orning
2 2 2 forks to hold the ridge pole of 5 1/2 foot abv Deck
3 3 3 Base [?] with a eye to hold the poles to stretch the orning 5 feet
4 the Joint of the Mast & hook for it to Lay in
T[hose] is pins to row by

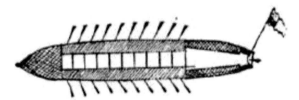

Clark's drawings of the Keelboat, Side Elevation, and Deck Plan. See Document 7.

		Boat 51 feet in Hold	Inches	
3 men takes up 3 feet		do 14 do on Cabin	32 Long	a Bench [?]
		do 8–4" wide	22 wide	

Lockers, must be 2 foot [?] – 6 In wide
do – k – 31 feet Long   196 foot of Plank a [one word illegible]
do about – 1 – 6 Deep   pr foot is

Lockers on the Cabin – 14 – 0 – long
do   Wide   3 – 0 – wide   84 feet
do   _____   3 – 0 – Deep

those who are heer right now. You'll meet the rest as time goes on." An that's just wut I did.

Normalee, wut day it is an such don't mean much ta me, but my joinin up with this expudishun seemed perdy important so I asked Captan Clark wut day it wuz wen I joined the Core. He tole me the date wuz Septembr 15, 1804. It was my birthday, of all things! So now I kin remembr and tell others about it. That's why I am beginin my Jurnul today.

I seen other fellas like Sarjunt Ordway an Pat Gas ritin down stuf in Diaryz of there own, an it seems like a good idee, so I am startin doin it too.

Everbody seemz like family here amongst the Core. Men I saw as strangers yesterday are like bruthers taday. I heer tell they had a few problems with dissiplin in the reel early days, but that got straightened out quik enuf with strict militaree rules. There wuz a cuple of kort marshals, an the fellas who wuz gilty got a whippin on there bare backs, as wuz the regl'r rules of the Army. Two of em stuck around an still serve with us today, but the other fella giv up an went back where he come frum, I guess. Now days we all watch out fer each other, tend to one another's needs, an everbody duz there share of the werk. Nobody would even think of tryin ta get outta doin their job or pullin their shift.

This is just like the Army in that respect. When a order is given, it's carried out staitaway. Nobody talks back ta them wuts in charge.

    I likes it heer! Makes me not miss people back home neer so much. I got new folks and bruthers heer, not just frends. Even the Captans are on perty much an even level with the rest of us. Yeah, theyz in charge an everone knows it, but they duzn't pull rank very often, an only wen reely necesary. They sets a good example of leedership, I thinks. Neether of em wood tell somebody ta do somthin they woodnt do their own selves. An neether of em is too high an mighty ta git down an dirty with the rest of us as we werk are way West. Everbody shares in both the good times an the hard times, an we woodnt have it any other way.

    Wile I'm thinkin on it, I need ta rite that I'll do my best ta include sum of the sights and feelins I git as I go on this heer jerney. Wen a fella duz this kinda thing all his life, it gits ta be second nature to him, an he kinda loses sight of the fact that people who never been out heer have no idee wut life is like out in the wild. We're plannin on goin wear no wites have ever been afer, so that leeves a lot ta rite about, don't it? I'll try ta picture my Momma readin this sum day an mebbe she'll get the same feelins I do wile I go on this long, great journey.

 Tother night at camp, I overheerd Captan Clark ask Captan Lewis somethin about them goin over Bujit ~ wutever that meens ~ somethin ta do about money, I'd gess. Lewis tole him not to wory about it. He sed the Prezident had gived him $2500 to go on this mission, and even if we wuz ta go over that amount, he had an open letter of credit to cover any extra expenses we run into. That seemed ta settle the matter fer Captan Clark.

{Subsequent to the end of the travels of the Corps of Discovery, the final tally for the overall cost of the mission was over 15 times the allotment Congress had granted them. The sum total was $38,722.35.
see Duncan, Dayton, & Ken Burns, *Lewis & Clark: The Journey of the Corps of Discovery*, pg. 12}

As we ben werkin are way upstream frum where I joint up, the first bunch of Injuns we come acros was sum folks I had already met afer. Theyz called the Hidasa, and are reel frendly. We stayed with em just a few days, then we moved on on akounta to the Captans time is gettin short afer winter sets in. The Hidasa gived us a great welcome, an we wuz reel glad that nice folks like them wuz the first Injuns we'd met. We figger there'll be ruffer gangs ahead of us, so this wuz a reely good beginin. They wuznt surprized at all ta meet wite peeple, as theyd alredy met a lot of travelers an trapers out thisaway. Most of em wuz Frenchees, though. Not too many Americuns, but there wuz quite a few Englishers out heer, as well.

Today as I was trackin a deer alongside the riverbank, I suddenly heered someone shout, "Hey there, Danny, git away from the edge like that! Come here this instant!"

Right away I turned to my left an ran back toward where the voice was comin from. It was Captan Lewis, an he had a stern look on his face.

"Danny, you gotta stay clean away from the edge like that. The bank of the river is covered with loose gravel an dirt, an it can give way beneath you at any second. You heer me?"

"Yes Sir, an thankee Sir," I replied. Thinkin about it a second, I sed, "Kin I ask, how did you know about that?"

The Captain glanced down toward his feet fer a moment, shook his head slowly a bit, then looked back up at me.

"Son, I know cause it happened to me, not long after we begun this jerney west. I was hykin along, mindin my own bizness, when in an instant I found myself sliding wildly down the edge of the high, steep riverbank. Ifn I hadn't quickly grabbed hold of a root that was stickin out, I coulda got hurt reel bad, or mebbe fallen into the river itself an drowned. That's how I know. So you be more careful~like from now on, ya heer?"

"Yessir," I replied, "I will." It got me ta thinkin how blessed of God is our Company, that our smart, kind Leader hadn't been killed back then. 'Thankee, God,' I thot to myself. 'Thankee very much.'

It looks like I pickt a heck of a time to join the Core, since the next tribe we come upon wuz the Lakota Soo. Theyz a real tuf bunch, ta put it mildly, always pickin fer a fight, and we neerly giv em one. They're theeves and pirates, forcen folks to pay em for travelin on the Mizura River. They're jest bullies, an they try ta wup everbody into payin them fer somethin that aint theirs ta own. The Captans stood up to em strait off tho, an told them that this wuz all U.S. teritoree now. They had no right to demand anything from us, ceptin our frendship, wich we wuz willin ta give. After that they seemd ta back off a little, but the Captans told us not to turn our backs on em fer a second. Next thing ya know, they sudenly tried to steel our botes, and we had to threten ta shoot em ifn they didn't back down. I don't know if they realized what cood happen to them if we fired our rifles, but they were mighty menacing, like shootin could break out any secund. Finly, all of a sudden, with a signal frum there cheef, they just up an left us alone, sayin they'd leev us be ifn weed let some of their womenfolk an children come abord the flatbote fer a looksee. Captan Clark thot that wuz ok, so they did. We had ta spend a couple more dayz neer em, but had to watch our stuf all the time fer feer they'd rob us, like theyd thretnd to do afer. They're a wicked, wicked bunch of savages! We finaly took off back up the Mizura, an none to soon, if ya ask me!

Weev bin camped alongside the river fer a week now because of terrible wether. Soon after I joined up with the Core, I had sent off a letter to my family through a trapper who happened to be crossing our path. Now, in an amazing stroke of luck, one of the fellas I had lernt my skills with met up with us wile we was stuck out here in the bad wether. He brought along with him a letter from my folks, jest in case he ever caught up with me. Aint God good?

David L. Miller

Oktober 1804

My Dear, Dear Son,

I have thot of you and prayed for you every single day, since you moved away. It is my fondest hope that God is takin good care of you, an that He is meeting your every need.

Its been a ruff year here on the farm. The sun scorched the corn til it burnt up an wuz useles, an the other vegetables wuz lost to. But jes like He did with the children of Izral in the wilderness, giving the people manna an quale, God provided an abundance of venison, turkee, rabitz, skwerly, an even sum buffalo fer us to eat an be satisfide. Prayz His Name! God is so good to us, even when we least deserve it.

Lots of people ask about you wen we see em, an we tell them we think yer doin ok. Since we haint herd nuthin, we hope that meens yer doin well. We got yer letter saying you were joining up with Captains Lewis an Clark. Iz Mr. Clark any relation to Gin'l George Rogers Clark? If so, youve made a good frend. We got no idee where you might be any more, but we pray this letter catches up with you in God's good time. That Summers girl who had her eye set on you, asks about you all the time. She's a rite fetchin young thing, an you cood do a lot worse, thats fer sur. I know she's six years younger than you, but what's a few years? Still, she's got a beau back thisaway, an if you dont come back soon, you may looze yer prize.

All of us back in Kentuckee send our luv. Your Opa, brothers Simon, Robert, Andrew, an Philip, and your sisters Ruth, Martha, Relehah, Sarah and Cassie send there hellos to. Take good care of yourself. Rite wen you can ifn this letter catches up with you, an no we are always thinken an praying for you everyday.

Luv, Mama

A Travelerz Trew Tale

    I probly ought ta mention somethin I take fer granted, but most of the rest of the fellers think is horibl, is the skeeters. Back east, the skeeters is bad enuf, but out thisaways theyz hundruds of timez wurse, bein like clouds thick around our hedz an such. The sky is gray with em sometimez, theyz so thick. We smeer bare grease all over us to keep em off durin the day, an Captan Lewis has with him wut he calls "skeeter nets" ta cuver us at nite. Even Captan Lewis's dog, Seeman, howls nite after nite frum all them bug bites. They sure make a body downright mizerabl. I cant tell ya how horrible it is out heer ~ them little buggers is jest everwears!

    I shud also talk a litle about the wildlife hereabouts, since thats a big part of wut this Core is all about ~ lernin all there is ta know about life out heer in the west, an tellin fokes back home

about it, speshuly Prezident Jefersun. The critters we come across is many an dyvers. Theyz all kinds of birds, bugs, animuls, lizerds, an such that no white man has seen or reported about afer. Captan Lewis is reel careful to rite about em all, an either skin em or save some of em live fer the Prezident to git a look see. He's to observe an make drawings of anything and everything new we discover out thisaways, which he is prompt to do. If'n he cant get a live or even a dead specimin, heez sposed to make a detailed drawing of it fer the Prezident.

A Travelerz Trew Tale

One of the oddest animuls we has discuvered is a critter we call a praree dog. It looks kinda like a rabit and kinda like a rat, only without a bushee tale or a long tale, jest a stubee one. It sits uprite an kinda barks or chirps when it gets upset, which is ofun. There are thousands an thousands of em out heer, like a huge swarm of cute little things, with holes in the ground all over the place. We dug into one of their buros fer hours an hours, an in the end tried to drown em out, which is what finaly werkd. Lewis skined one and kept another one alive fer Mr. Jefersun.

We even runned into a huge kinda bare, diferent than weed ever seed afer. We called it a White or Grizlee bare. It kin take a duzun or more rifle shots an stil not fall down an die! Insted it jest gets madder an madder, unless ya shoot it in the head. It dint take us long ta lern ta give em a wide berth; jest leev em be, unless we wuz reely hungry or they wuz threatinin us. Many are the stories we have of encounters with such monsters, however. They may be terrible hard ta kill, but the meet is mighty fine eatin.

 Seemz like all we ever duz is row, pole, or dress out the hides of the animuls we kilt the day afer. Tiz an ongoin job, but we'll need them hides fer warmth an protection from the wind an rain an snow come reely cold wether. Polin the flatbote is a job I woodnt force on my worst enemy. The bote can get all snarled up on trees, roots an branches stickin up outa the water, or even worse, hiden underneeth the surface. We gots ta rassle are way free without dumpin the bote, are supplies, an areselves into the mudee River, wich is often fast an deep. A feller cood drown hizself iffin he wuznt reel

David L. Miller

careful. Any man will get very tired out heer, werkin hard as can be ta drive the keelbote an canoos upstreem against the currant. Are hands an arms an backs an even are legs get tired from hour after hour of strainin agin the oars an poles, or towin the botes with ropes. Not only is it extreemely hard werk, but its frightful cold, too. Even in summer, the Mizura water is cold. The mud is sticky, soze we need to tromp in the River without our mocasins on, or else weed lose em. That makes it even colder than if we at least had em on fer a bit of warmth. Its a neverendin job, but its wut we gotta do soz we can go further north an West to the Pasific Oshun, wich is are gole.

　　Its Fall now an tother day we met up with another tribe of Injuns. These is called the Arikara peeple, and are quite nice. The Captans gave speeches an

handed out prezunts, like the Peese Medle with Prezident Jefersun's pitchr on one side an with two fellers shakin hands on the other, meenin frend or peese. The Injuns got all kinds of other stuff frum us like beads an ribuns an such, wich makes em all perdy hapy. Seems that they enjoy licker a lot, too ~ too much fer there own good most of the time. I seem ta recall heerin about Injuns back yeers ago havin the same trubl. They sure likes their booz, an thats a fact! But it gets em all riled up an fystee, which is somthin we definitly dont need along the way. Weez out heer ta make new frends, not enemies, so we dont give the Injuns guns or wisky or other stuff thatd get em mad at us or ryled up somehows. The Captans dont trade or give the licker out ifn they dont have to, or unless we're celubratin somthin speshul.

One of the tribes of Injuns Prezident Jefersun espeshuly

wants us to get to be frends with is the Mandan Injuns. Theyz the ones we come acros next, further on up the River, an they is as frendly as weed hoped theyd be. The Captans had expected ta be at the mouth of the Mizura by this time, but we aint, so theyz desided weed best stay here with these Injuns durin the cold munths. So we is bilding us a fort here, wich we call Fort Mandan, after themuns.

Sinse we been here, we met a fella named Tusant Sharbono and his two wives. He claimz ta be a

good interperter, as well as a hunter an traper. One of his wives, named Sakajuweea, is real pregnunt. Sheez such a youngin, too ~ probly about 15 or so! But smart as a wip. His tother wife is gonna stay here with the

Mandans when the rest of us plan ta keep on goin. Sakajuweea had herself the baby wile we been here amung the Mandans. The boy's name is John Bapteest but Captan Clark got us all ta callin him Pomp. The three of em is plannin on goin with our Core wen we leave, an weez glad ta have em. I think Sakajuweea is a better Injun-talker than her man. Personally, I thinks he is kinda lazy and a big talker with nuthin much ta back it up. He claims a lot of good stuff about hisself that he can't follow thru on wen the goin gits tough.

 One of the most importunt things Captan Clark keeps werkin on wile weer at Ft Mandan is a deetaled map of the U.S. an the lands we have cuvered so far. He noz Prezident Jefersun is espeshuly interested in such like, so hez doin a real good job of it. He also is ritten about 53 Mizura River tribes hereabouts, like the

Injuns tole him there is.

    One of the funiest things I ever seed wuz the Mandans carien on over Captan Clarks slave, York. Seemz like theyd never seed a blacky afer, an they kept rubbin on him to try an get the dark skin color ta come off. Slaves they know about, sinse some of them is slaves to other tribes, an some other tribes is slaves to the Mandans, but this heer black fella wuz holy new to em. Seein white men is funy enuf around heer, let alone a blacky. We in the Core take him fer granted, as he aut to be, an he werks reel hard, liken he aut to, so we all gets along with him just fine. He obays his Master Clark jest like he shud, so he dont make no truble fer anybodee. In fact, I think he werks even harder than sum of us'uns, ta tell the truth. It wuz such a funy site tho, ta see them Injuns carien on like that, let me tel you.

Onst we got our fort bilt heer at Ft Mandan, we settled in fer the winter. Seemz like Spring, wen we can muve on, is never gonna come. Its terribl cold and even snowee sometimes, gettin as low as 45 dugreez below zero. But wen the wether gits bad an the snow is deep an the cold is bitter, itz teribl rough goin. The dry icy wind blows right through a man, and woah to the fella who has ta stand guard duty at night.

Most of the time we have good eatin, speshuly the bufalo, elk, an deer that is in great abundunce. We kin eat mebee nine pounds or more of meet every day an still be hungree. That's caus therez not much fat in the meet. An we werks reel hard every day, which gives a feller a mitey big appetite.

Nuther thing weer doin to keep areselves busy and warm wile weer at Ft Mandan is to dig out some new canooz fer us to take as we head furthur upriver.

I gotta say, we are havin a pleasant time these munths among the Mandans. I think we has made sum frends. We has all dun are best to be good to the Injuns and let them be good to us to wile we is heer. During these long cold munths we has lotsa time ta talk. Some of the stuff they has told us includes that they're lookin forward to are return. They giv us directions an ideas about who and wut we might find ahead of us. We is grateful ta have a place ta hang on in until the winter finally subsides, realizing that to hed out too early wood be jest plain foolish. We are relatively sheltered at the fort. To take off fer the West afer the werst of the wether was past cood leave us unexpectedly stranded in deep snow, horrible wind, and bitter temperatures. We jest have to wait, like it or not.

One of the very difficult things about livin out heer in the frigid cold is the matter of goin to the latrine. We git all dressed up ta go out an "do our duty" as nature intended, but many of us neerly get frostbit in the time we is out there. Some of usuns try ta hold it off as long as we kin to avoid the bitter cold, but a body kin only hold out so long afer we git sick frum waitin too long. A body cood literaly freez his butt off in this horrid wether. We jest have ta go an do it, eventually.

One of the things I lernd wile we wuz at Ft. Mandan wuz that the Core didn't actually begin at St Loois as I had imagined. They had left that place as their "starting point," but Captan Lewis had taken a grate deel of time before the trip traveling all up an down the east coste lernin frum experts about stuff he would need ta know during the jerney of explorashun. He had started out as Prezident Jeferson's secretary, and even then started lernin things. As time grew neerer fer the actual trip ta begin, Captan Lewis sought out the knowledge of a grate many men soze he cood succeed in the mission. He went frum Montichello to Washingtun, to Harpers Ferry, Virginny, ware he bought the 1803 guns and small cannon weed have on the keelbote. He went on ta Philadelfia an other places soze he cood keep alernin important things.

Well, we has lerned all we kin frum the Injuns about wut lays ahead of us, an then lo these many munths, we are finaly headin west fer are destinashun. I gotta say, fer savages, they hav acted neer like Christians, though they had no god we cood speak of.

Jest before we left the Mandans, we sent the keelbote back down the Mizura to St Loois, with All the Stuff we had colected so far, fer Mr Jefersun an others ta studee. Sum of the Core members went back with are spesumins, an all the rest of us headed upriver toward the mountuns an the western sea. Captan Lewis hopes we is perty close to the mountuns, an we shouldn't take too long frum here on in to get to the Pasifik Oshun. We left Ft Mandan on April 7, 1805, spektun ta be back thisaways by this time next yeer.

As we is travelin, one of the danjers we run up agin is the shore line of the river itself. The water rushes down streem, wearin away the soft, sandy dirt along the river's edge and without warning, a hole huge bank of the riverside will come crashin down into the water. Captan Lewis tells me this is called "Eroshun," an happens naturully, wether by wind or water. Ifn we or are botes are too close to the edge of the river, the downslide cood hurt us reel bad, an almost has a couple of timez.

Recently, a thing that happened to us on are way wuz wen we neerly lost a lot of importunt papers an instruments when a canoo neerly tipped over. Sakajuweea wuz quik to rescue the things before they cood get away downstreem or sink out of site. It wuz her man wut tipped the canoo, an he wuz too scared ta get it back uprite. The Captans wuz terrible angry with him, but neither of them wuz aboard that canoo at the time, soz they couldn't place too much blame on him. Wut had happened wuz we sudenly come to a fork in the River. Shood we go one way or tother? Sumbudy yelled to him as loud as they could, but it all happened too quick to do much about it, and the stuff wuz spilled. If it hadn't been for the squaw, most of the Captans' hard werk wooda bin lost.

Walkin alongside the River aint much better a lot of the time. The tall thik grasses an weeds cling to are clothes and act like they dont want us ta take one more step forward. Wile the wether up heer in these Dakota lands is rarely extra~hot, the sun beats down on us an makes it feel a lot hotter with all our geer on than ifn we didn't have ta carry it all. But we know that it'll all be needful onest we get into the colder lands to the west of us. That dont make the burden any easier, but at least we have a good rezun fer the back~braking labor we have ta endure every mile of the way. When the sun is full an hot on are backs, we think about all the trees we miss frum back east. Out heer on the open praree therez nary a tree to be seen fer miles around most of the time. Quite a ways back it seemed like we would never get away from the thik growth of trees an undergrowth, but out heer its nothin but wide open spaces an a fella kin see fer milez around in all directions. Thats good fer keepin our eyes peeled fer Injuns an such, but it makes the jerney seem ferever unending.

Anuther storee wuz wen we got to a fork in the River and we wuznt sure which was the real Mizura. The Captans tole us we shud make are choice, sayin wether we thot either way wuz the rite one. Most of us sed our piece, an the grater number thot we shud hed north. Captan Lewis sensed we oughta go on the south branch ~ like mebee it wuz the Real Mizura ~ but the rest of us had all chose ta go on the north branch. The two men

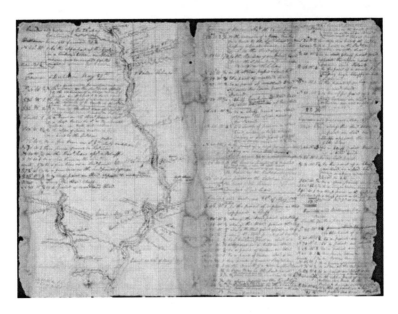

talked it over butween themselves an desided ta go there separate ways, an none of us even fussed. They had brought us this far ok; why shood we doubt em now? Two seperate parties tried the North and South forks, and eventually it turned out that the Southern route was the right one indeed. So we went North fer quite a while, an shur nuff, the ones wut went South wuz rite, an we wuz rong.

Once we wuz all headed South together, the river meandered fer quite a spell and soon we cood heer a rushing, deafening sound

ahead. One of the places the Mandans had tole us wuz comin up soon wuz a place they called the Grate Falls of the Mizura. I gotta admit, most everthin they tole us we took with a grane of salt, since we dint no wut wuz fer reel an wut wuz just there imajunashun, but them Falls sur was a fact.

Just afer we got there tho, we come acros some windee, sandee lands that neerly ripped us apart as we traveled. The blowin sand

got in are faces, eyes, ears, an mouths an we cood hardly breeth sumtimez. Lukulee we dint have to stay in that area too long. But I'll tell you, them Grate Falls wuz Grate indeed! I never seen anythin like it in all my daze. They wuz Butiful an real Powerful ~ you kin tell just by watchin em. We had to portaj them hollowed-out log canooz around the falls, an it wuz heavy werk, but we got it dun, jest like we do every time we haf to.

    Once we got around the immense region of the Grate Falls, wich took about 4 weeks, we got ready to canoo some more. Captan Lewis had had a iron canoo bilt afer we came West, an we cuverd it with elk an bufalo skins to keep it aflot. But it dint werk. The seams leek'd caus we dint have no pitch or tar, an the bote sank right down to the bottom of the River. We cood tell Captan Lewis felt reel teribl

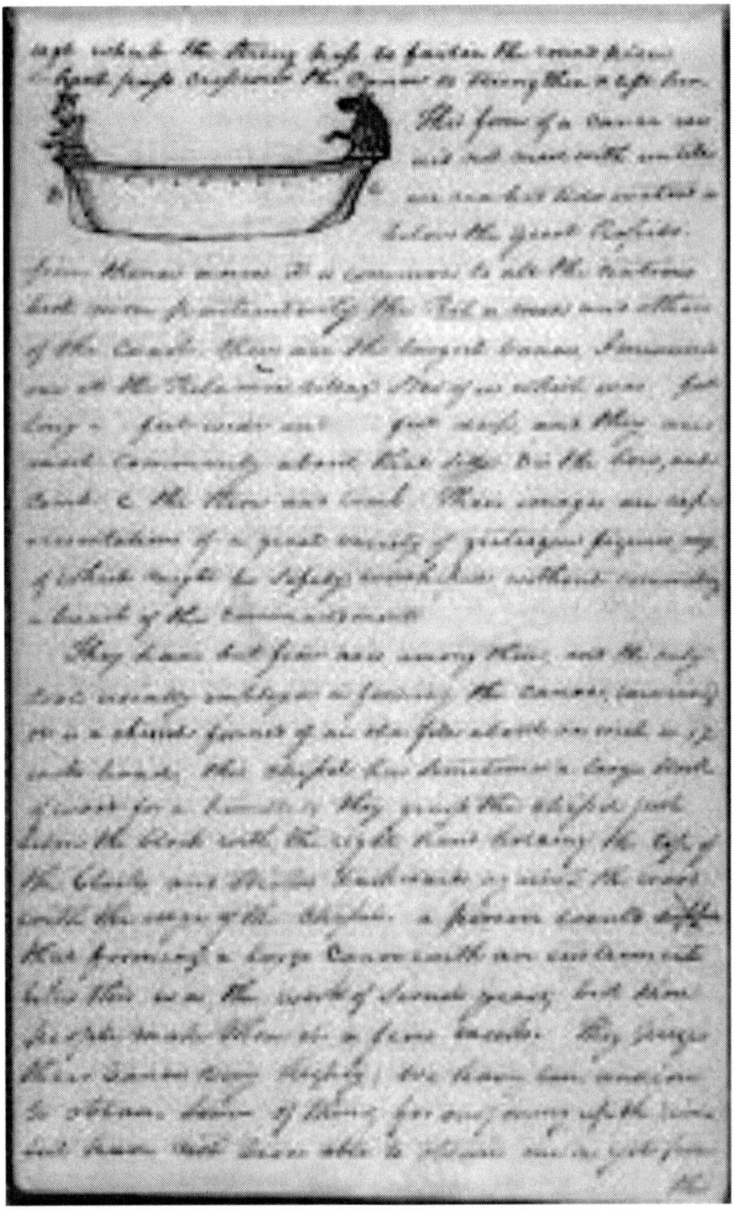

about his lost bote, that he wuz shur would werk, but it sank like a stone. Nobody sed narry a werd, tho ~ not one werd. We just went on with the botes we had, an made some more canooz soonez Captan Clark could find some good cottonwoods. All in all, it took us a whole munth ta travers those rapidz.

I thinks the werst part of the portaj an a lot of the marchin around heer is that there is a wild plant that we call the pricklee pare, an weev got em fer most of the rest of the hike until we git to the mountuns. We cant help but step on em, an they stick right up thru are mokasuns, an hurt are feet sumthin teribl! Not only do they hurt at the time we step on em, the holz in our feet get ta bleedin an infektud, an it is awful hard ta even walk. This here reminds me of the Old Testamint story of how the Children of Izral walked through the wilderness for 40 yeers but their sandals never wore out! Weer all the time havin ta either repair or replace ours, good as we kin make em. So it sounds to me like them Izralites had mighty fine sandals or a mighty fine God...probably both. All in all, it took us a whole munth ta traverse those rapidz!

  I cant say this stronglee enuf ~ narry a step of this expudishun is eezy. Wether we is too hot or too cold, too hungree or too sick, even Captan Lewis's sad timez arnt enuf ta keep us frum

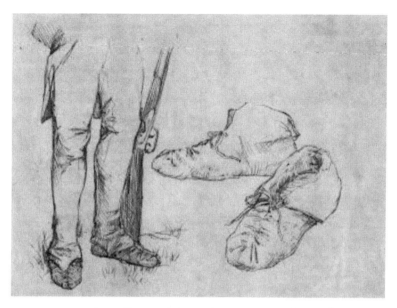

are goal. But it shur as heck isnt eezy! Many is the time we gets disceraged, an sum of us wish there is a easier way to go, but we still keeps on followin the Captans, cause we knows they got the Goal in mind all the time, an are best interests at hart.

One of the smartest things the Captans did wuz bring along just enuf wisky an tobakee as ta get us far away frum civilizashun afer we ran out, soz nobody cood turn back til it wuz too late. I don't go in fer wisky much, but I like my pipe frum time ta time. After the tobakee rund out, we went with sum weeds the Injuns call Kunikunik.

    There wuz one time Sakajuweea got teribl sik, teribl bad off, with cramps an fever an chills, so it lookd like she wuz a goner. Captan Clark bled her an all, but still she didn't get better. We all felt bad fer her and fer Pomp too ~ he coodnt figer out why his Mama wuz cryin an fussin so. In time, after Captan Lewis gave her herbs, evenshully she pulled thru, which we were awful glad about, him espeshully.

    As I looks back on the stuf I writ so far, I makes it sound like we dont have no fun at all durin this Jurney. That jest aint trew. I shud rite that therez always time fer jawin even wile weer werkin. Sum of the fellers is particularlee good story tellers, an that makes the time go a lot faster, it seemz. Therez timez wen we git ta singin an dancin to the fiddle wen the time is rite.

    Even Captan Lewis gets into it sumtimez an tells us sum stories about the time wile he wuz Mr. Jeffersun's studunt afer the man becum Prezident, an later wile servin as his Secerteree. The Prezident lerned him all kinds a stuf that heed be needin come time fer this trip. Not only did he train Captan Lewis persunally in varius subjects, but he even sent him to skools

thruout Europe an Amerika ta study up on sciens, math, starlookin, mapmakin, an medisun, an they talked about the kind of hopes an dreams the Prezident has fer our trip. It wuz Mr. Jefersun wut come up with the name fer our teem, "the Core of Discuvery." Captan Lewis already knew a lot about bein in the outdoors, so he kin fend well fer hisself an the rest of us.

    The Prezident speshuly emfasized that he wants us ta make as many Injun frends as we can thruout are travels. He dont necesarily like em or trust em, but he wants ta know all he can about there thinkin an ways of life, so he can better understand em. One of his golez is ta make the West free an open fer ferther western growth an trade fer us wites, so we kin spred out an not be confined jest to the east coste. Sinse weez got areselves as far as the Misisipi, wut lies beyond? How much ferther kin we go? Wut kind of land is out there? Mr. Jefersun seems like a man with one big queshun after anuther. We hopes ta anser as many of em as we kin.

Theez flat praree lands jest seem ta go on and on ferever. It seems like a never ending jerney, wether weer hikin on land or in the water, canooin or polin the botes. Botes wut we call canoos, Sharbono calls "peerogz"

or some such thing in his Frenchee language. I can't understand him half the time, but both Captans know how to speak "Frog" like he does so I guess that's all that matters to me. Anyways, wether weer on land or in the water, the area we have ta cross is vast ~ further than I ever cooed have imagined when we first started.

Last night, just before we wuz gonna turn in and get some shut eye, I saw Sargent Gass writing in his Diary about the progress of the Core. I made my way over to him and asked, "Ya mind if I look it how you rite things down in yer Jernal?" He shook his head, gave me a smile and said, "No, go rite ahead, I don't mind a bit." He handed over the stack of pages and I began to try my best to read as much as I could of em. First off, I noticed that he put dates and days of the week with every entry, while I had left that part

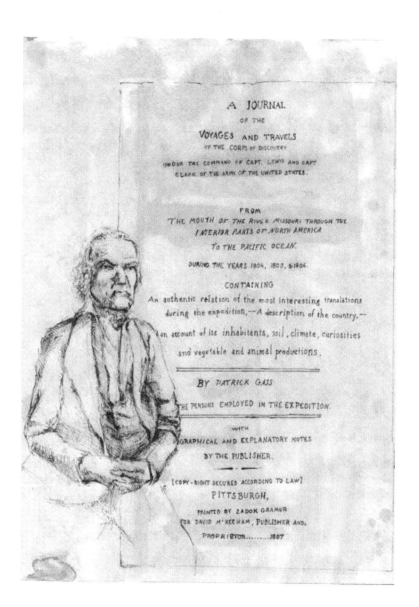

out. I sure did like seein how he writ his jernal.

I thinks a little different about dates though, than Gass does. They don't matter much to me. As it says in the Good Book, "The Good Lord knows what we have need of and He supplies all are needs. If He feeds the birds of the air and takes care of all the flowers that bloom so beautifully all around us every day, what do we have to worry or complain about?" So I jest take one day at a time and let that dayz troubles take care of themselves.

Our over~land Party, who wuz hikin with Captan Lewis, come upon the Shoshonez, a bunch we also called the Snake Injuns. They wuz kinda shy of us at furst, but Captan Lewis got em ta trust us. He aproched them with no gun or wepons at all, jest his open hands. They cood have killed him strate off, but he trusted em, and wanted them ta know it. Come ta find out, there chief turned out to be the very Brother of Sakajuweea! Her yunger sister was there too. Needlus to say, we got a grand welcum frum them. The three of em had a Very Grate Reuniun, an we talked to em fer a long time. We spent quite a spell with em, getin to know em wile we waited fer Captan Clark an the botes ta catch up with us. We ended up spendin a couple a weeks amongst em, lernin their ways an seein how they lived. They had many different ways of thinkin about things, such as how many wives a fella cood have ~ shucks, I think one wood be more than enuf fer me! They even let sum of are Core stay in there tents, them thinkin it wood be "good Majic" fer them to have us sleepin amung em. We found out that many of the Injun tribes felt the same way.

Onest we wuz finally settin out fer the West agin, they give us all the extra horses they cood spair, an one of the Injuns, a hunter of therez that we called "Old Toby," came along with us to show us a shortcut thru the mountans. It wuz our hope to go straight frum the Mizura on to the Sammun River, and frum there on to the Culumbia, but Toby warned us it couldn't be dun that strataways.

As we get further and further West, the flat land is slowly getting more and more hilly, with even some low mountans. We left the source of the Mizura back a few days ago. At one point, where the Mizura River begins, a cuple of us straddled the starting point ~ a mere trickle comin up outta the ground! It wuz exciting to behold. We then buried the canooz so we cood use em agin ifn we want to when we head back home. Now it's up to usuns to carry are loads on are backs or on the backs of the horses. Man, if we hadn't run into Sakajuweea's bruther and his Tribe, weed have been in for reel trouble, what with all the materials we is bringin along.

    Sumthin jest okured ta me that I oughta mention. Out heer, wen we travel overland, we sumtimez go fer quite a spell without running into any water. Wen that happens, we get ta smellin perdy bad. We can't help it, between bein sick frum time ta time, bein out in the hot sun, an all the werk we has ta do, carryin are packs an such. So wut we do insted of washing with water, we rub the sandy, dry dirt over are bodies, an kinda scrub the smell away. We areselves don't notice it much, since weer so used ta one another, but a lot of timez it makes it hard ta hunt, cause the animuls kin smell are sent frum a grate distance. This area has so many buffalo there like bees on a hunny tree. There's so many thousands we cant begin ta count em. Wen they git startled, there hoofbeats sound like terrible thunder, roarin an rumblin across the wide, vast, open praree.

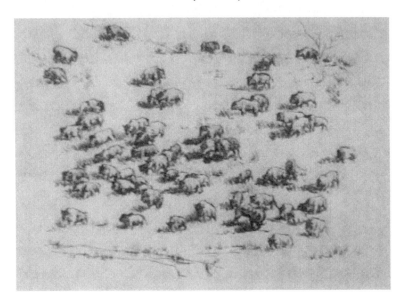

Not only is the lay of the land getting higher and more difficult to hike uphill, but the wether is gettin colder, too. I thought I had left the worst of winter behind us back with the Mandans, but heer weer headin into it again, it seems. Actually, Captan Lewis explained to us that winter is still a ways off, it's just because weer getting higher into the sky that it's getting colder. We can see the snow an ice on the distant mountans ahead of us, and the sight isn't a plesant one.

    As we git closer and closer to the mountans, the Captans have had us stop and dig big, deep holes in the ground so we could "cash" some of our stores and belongings for the return trip ~ whenever that might be. We laid aside some of our guns, powder, and lead so we cood defend areselves on the homeward jerney. We're gettin a bit low on trinkets and beads for the Injuns, but we put aside a few of them things too, in case we need ta trade or make frends with new folks. The rest weer carryin with us as we travel further West.

Before we kin get to the West coste, we have to hassle with them mountuns first. That was reel hard news fer us. Eventually, after a awful hard time, we got thru the Biterroot Vally and into the Mountuns themselves, but somehow we missed the shortcut Old Toby had been lookin for. Onest we Finaly got to them gosh awful big Mountuns, we thot we wer gonna die fer sur! Weed thot the Apalashuns wuz big ~ but shoot, they wuz nuthin but hilloks compared to these Monsters! We cud see em from ferever far away, an they seemed to reech Hi as the Sky. It is hard an dangerus climin. There wuz jest no ways we cood go over em, Ida figerd. But sure nuff, Captans Lewis an Clark, they found a way. Sakajuweea has helped em a lot. An Old Toby, too. That Injun girl seemz ta know jest about everthin a body needs ta know ta travel out this aways.

Captan Lewis says that he an Prezident Jefersun calls these the Grate Rockee Mountans, an I kin totally agree with em ~ they sure IS rockee! Theyz immensely tall an a feller kin see em fer hundurds of milez away. They fills up the hole sky with there imensity. They're rough, an have snow up the sides an on top, even wen its not winter, which it aint quite yet. Weel be doin all we kin do ta git across em afer winter duz set in! The big problem is, no one knows jest how far across they run. They cood be a short span, or a reely fer peece. Weel jest haf ta find out.

In sum places we have to leev the horses behind cause the path is too narrow. Thatz when we get to eat a good meal fer a change, cause the horses would die out here on there own, soz we shoot em an eat em to fill our bellies up some. That aint as bad

as it sounds. Other than then, many is the timez we is almost starvin ta deth, an it gets so cold we reely wished we cood go back home or jest plain up an die fer reel.

Now that weer gettin up higher into the Rockees, we gets ta thinkin theres no further way ta go, but somehow we manages ta find a way. The cold is so teribl that iffin we goes out of our tents fer only a cuple of minutes at a strech, we neerly freez areselves. Sumtimez a feller dont wanna get out of his tent in the mornin, its so cold. It took him so long ta get the dang thing set up in a way thats safe, an then the wind an snow comes along an buries the thing totuly under. Jest wen ya think you'll get sum good rest an sleep fer a wile, sumbudy comes along an digs ya out an wakes ya up ta pull guard an sentree dutee, or keep the camp fires stocked with wood.

    Other timez we gotta go out early in the mornin ta find food fer the rest of the men. Bein so high up in the Mountans in the biter cold, animuls are hard ta

find ~ leest ways enuf fer the hole Core. All we see is mountain gotes an pronghorn antelop, an even them is rare. Because meet is so hard ta come by, we hav had ta shoot the horses an eat them, like I wrote afer. It meens weel haf ta cary all the stuff the horses wuz carryin.

The peaks of these Rockee Mountans are glorious an wonderful, bitter~sharp an evil, all at the same instant. They are

lovely an barren, rapturous an deadly at every turn. As we go up thru the Mountans, many is the time we come to an area that looks like there is a good spot ta pass thru, but insted it turns out ta be completely blocked with deep, deep snow, an is impasabl. It gits so disceragin!

    Now we come to an area we call the Lolo Stream. It's carryin us quicker down out of the mountans than weed been goin afer. There are rocky falls along the way that we haf ta portaj, but fer the most part its easier sailin, gliding downstream. I finally decided that I woodn't rite so much during these timez in the mountans ~ it's jest too cold fer my face an fingers.

    A cuple of things I lerned from Captan Lewis is that the air up heer is so hard ta breeth because of our "elervation" ~ that meens being high in the sky. The air gits thinner the higher we climb, an though the werk stays the same, plodding on mile after mile, the hite an cold makes the werk all the more mizerabl. Not only is the air thin an the wether teribl cold, but the march thru the deep snow is mighty hard on us. We need ta be verry careful wherever we put our feet. Ya never kin tell if the snow underneeth ya is gonna hold or give out. Unexpected "quiksand~like" snow kin suddenly surprise ya, an afer ya know it, yer neck deep in snow, ifn not over yer hed! We keep watchin out fer one another soz nobody gets lost in the depths of the snow, an despite sum close calls, we been safe so far.

The trails we manage ta find are extremely steep an icy, an both areselves an the horses we still have find it mighty hard goin. Time an agin the horses have tumbled down the mountanside, an some have been very hurt indeed. With every fall, we haf ta collect as many of the animals' pack belongings as we kin find, then load em back onto the horses if they are able ta carry em. Some of the horses have been too badly injured to carry on, so we have ta shoot em an have a number of meals from their bodies. It's sad, but it helps us keep up our strength.

 I cant say enuf how terrible, bitter cold it is up heer. We think back on where we been, back wen the sun beat down on us an neerly fried us to a crisp sometimez. But up heer it aint nuthin at all like that. Sure, there are days wen the sun shines like blazes, but we dont seem ta git any warmth frum it. But there are also a lot of timez, specially wen its snowin, which is often, that we never actually see the sun ~ therez jest the light of day ta lite are way. It makes the days seem a lot shorter because its hazy wen we wake up, an the light seems ta go out so much sooner without the open sun ta light up the sky.

Finally, after a long, hard, bitter cold clime, an with Sakajuweea's help, we got to meet up with the Nez Purse Injuns, who is a verry agreeable bunch. We iz stayin with em fer quite a spell afer weer muvin on West, soz we can regane our strength an gain back a little of our weight after loozin so terribl~much thru lack of food in the Mountans. Goin with hardly any food is more tough on a body than I kin describe. We need the strength ta keep pressin on, but without the energy that food an water provides, we got weeker minute by minute. The Core as a hole needs time like this with the Nez Purse ta help us recooperate an get redy fer the last leg of the Jerney. It seemz these Injuns eat mostly roots, berries, an whatever fish they can find, an that's about all. They made us a grand meal to celebrate our arrival, an we gorged arselves on the foods that were laid out before us. I dont know wether it was because we ate so much so fast, or because of the nature of the food, but nearly all of us got sick from it. It is takin us neerly a week or more to git over it. Captan Clark gave some of us Dr Rush's pills, to rid us of the poisons or whatever, but we have had a bad time of it fer a while. Weez all perdy weak an can hardly press on, soz now is gud a time as any ta take a brake fer a spell.

Surprizingly, the distance between the end of the Mizura an the beginning of the Snake River weren't too terribl fer apart. The Nez Purse, wen we left em, warned us of sum terrible rapids ahead of us, but we took em on an beat em, even though the

Injuns were sure weed have been killed in the attempt. We then had to pass though them enormous mountans, of course, but the actual distance in milez wasn't too far. After all this time we got onto wuts called the Cleerwater River, an frum there onto the Snake, an FINULY onto the Culumbia! Furthur West weev met up with even more Injun tribes, too. Theezuns are called the Flatheads [Salish], the Wanapams, the Yakimas, an the Walulas. I jest has ta ad this thot ~ Iz afeerd I problee fergot sum of them Injun tribez names, an wen exactly we met em, but I think I got sum of em. I jest had ta stick that in ther, so others kin git the hole trewth.

AT LONG LAST, on Novembr 7, 1805, Captan Clark tole us he reckoned we was perdy close to the Pasifik Oshun! But sadly, after the fog cleerd up sum, we lernt it wuznt the Pasific at all but just a big ol bay of the Culumbia. We all felt like we were so very close ta it yet oh so far away. It wuz mighty discouraging wen we came to that realization. Ta come so close an yet feel so far frum our objective!

It wernt too much longer that we actshuly seed the Pasifik tho, an lo wuz it a wonderful Site to behold! No sooner than we reached the Mighty Oshun than a bunch of us dropped our gear and flung areselves into the water for which we had striven so long. What a surprise we got! That water was freezin cold, an we dashed back for shore as quick or quicker than we had run into it!

Now that we had at last got to the Pasifik Oshun, Captan Lewis got ta figerin, an he gesed that the Core had traveled about 4162 miles sinse they left the

Misisipee River! (Cours I only went a porshun of that distanse with them, sinse I joint up a little later than the rest.)

Along the coast there is the Chinook, Clatsop, an Tilamook tribes, with the most frendly of them all bein the Clatsop bunch. Heerz where we had a big choice ta make. Should we build our fort on the north side of the Culumbia, which we called Cape Disappointment, or on the south side? The Captans coudnt decide

at the time which was better fer us in the long run. We might have a better chanse ta meet up with a incoming ship on the north side. But the south side is near wear the Clatsops live, an it mite be in our best interest to stick neer ta themuns. They finully decided we shud take a vote. As I understand it, this wuz <u>The Very First Time</u> a bunch of Americuns got to VOTE west of the Misisipee River! Neerly all the time, wutever the comanders sed was Gospel, but not in this case. In fact, every ONE of us got to vote, including our blacky and the Injun woman! Nobody else but Captans Lewis an Clark would ever have let a woman or espeshully a slave vote! The mujority of us desided to bild our fort on the South bank of the Culumbia, an we named it Fort Clatsop.

    We got most of the Fort dun just afer the snow hit ~ an nun to soon! We started it on

Fort Clatsop

December 7, 1805 and most of it wuz finished by Christmus Day. It was a speshul day fer all of us. We fired off the canon to honor the Christ child's birthday an even exchanged gifts with one another ~ just little mementoes to remember the event and keepsakes to honor our fellow Core members by. One of the fellas pulled out his fiddle an we all sang an danced in time to the music, ta celebrate. It wuz an awful good time together!

The wethr here is cold, snowy, rainy, an Verry, Verry Sokin Wet the hole time. Its ofun fogy an jest plain mizerabl most of the time. In fact, there is daze at a strech wen we cant even see the sun fer all the
thik fog, like the sun has dun gone out. Wen the deep, hevy snow comes, which is often, we jest haf ta hunker down an wait it out unless we absolutly haf ta have somethin outside the Fort. Weer tryin ta make the best of it wile we haf to stick it out heer on the West Coste, but everone is ichin to hed back East fer Home agin.

It's during our stay heer that Captan Clark has finuly finishd his map of the Unitud Stats, frum Coste to Coste, an he is as hapy as a songburd! He dezervz it too! Fer him to take all them mesurments an put it all tagether on one peece a paper is a mirakle ta behold!

Bein out heer with all this rain is both a blessing an a curse. We lerned right off that drinkin salt water makes us as sick as dogs. The water hits are stumacks an right away we start pukin. So we has ta stick with clean, pure streem water, not that of the oshun. But besides gettin rain water an such ta drink, the constant rain gets are clothes all wet, soze they rarely dry out, an frum that they git smelly with mildoo an mold. We try ta wash em out as best we kin, but until we hed back East agin, weer probly gonna haf ta jest live with it.

Wile weer out heer on the coste, Captan Lewis has been gettin hisself more an more depresed; teribl sad about sumthin ALL the time, but

A Travelerz Trew Tale

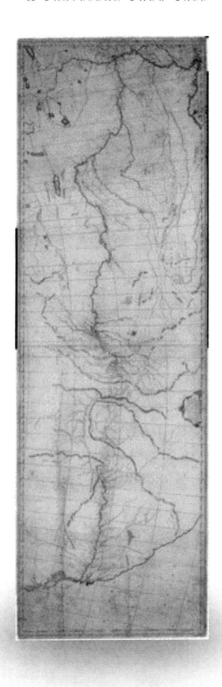

nobody noz wut fer. He barks at peeple, gets mad a lot, an sulks fer no rezun we noz of. All of us gots ta wate out the wether, Captan Lewis included, til it gets a bit warmer afer we can get are gear tagether an head fer Home.

During the time we are on the coste, we is usin are time wizely to the best of our abilities. There are thousands of sammun an various other fishes swimming along the coste, most of em thrashing upstream as tho the

very devil himself is trying to catch em! The Injuns around heer go out daily an catch or spear as many as they can, then skin an gut em, before smoking them over large wooden frames, to dry them out, for saving until later. To eat em, the Injuns boil em over an open flame, then load em up onto wooden slats or clay-hardened plates fer a hardy meal. When the wether is cleer enuf, we hed down the coste to where there is a huge cash of salt bildup on the shore of the ocean. We bring along pails, fill em with saltwater, an boil it down til only the dry salt remains.

Wile weer waiting fer the salt to boil off, we goes fishin. Sammun is mitey good eatin an are abundant as the herds of deer an bufalo we saw on the trip out thisaways. In case ya don't know, we need salt fer preserving all the meet an fish we kin catch, soz it won't go bad on us on the return trip. Everbody everwears needs salt in their diet ta keep em healthy, an we used up neerly all the salt we had brought along with us on the way West.

The Injuns told us of a large wale that had beached itself an died down the coste a ways. There was plenty of meat an blubber fer all of us ~ Clatsops an Core members alike. The fat was kinda rubbery, but not too bad to the taste.

The wether out heer is generally foggy and often cold, an I sure am glad we got the fort to

return to after a hard dayz werk out felling trees fer the warmth of the fire, fer boiling down the salt, an fer hollowin out new canooz fer the return trip. Forests are abundant and the trees straight an tall. The ship~rites back in the East would love to have material like theez to build masts an spars out of!

It's been so terribl long since we wuz home, I almost fergit wut it feels like. All of us is testy, an redy ta hed back to the areas we call Home, but the time still ain't rite yet. Sum of the men heer has wives and younguns back home, an ya gotta no it's hard on them to be away fer so long. Fer all they noze, we cood all be dead out heer in the wilderness. Still, the winter is lingering heer, and we know it's even worse in the mountans, so we jest gotta be pashunt. In the meantime, we scout up an down the coste, seeing new sites, meeting new tribes. The Captans busy thereselves ritin down all the details of our jerney, including drawings of birds, bugs, fish, plants, and animuls.

One day we wuz out huntin an wen we came back to the fort weed shot a cariboo, a mess of wild turkeys, an even a mule deer buck. We knew the fellas back at the camp would be plenty happy to have something different than fish to eat fer a change, and it would also be good to salt an save sum of the meat fer are trip back East. Sum of us go out ever day to shoot as much meat as we can before the time to leeve comes upon us. Not a one of us prefers to stay behind, that's fer sure! But at least we got lotsa good food ta eat, insted of neerly starving ta death like we did in them darn mountans on our way West.

Sarjunt Gass told me that according his Jernal, we been heer nearly five munths, an it has rained the hole time except fer but 12 days. It'll be so good ta be warm an dry agin.

Gradually, as the winter wether has started to cleer, the Captans are ordering us to gather up our things and prepare to moov out. Weev been buildin up to this time fer months now, and exsitement is in the aire. Weev managed, at grate cost to us in goods, to trade fer some horses ta git us on are jerney home, an the Injuns made out like theeves on the deel. But like it or not, we need the horses to get us back, so what's a body ta do? Day by day we load the packs that will soon be piled onto the horses' backs, as well as on our own. Some of our belongings will travel in the canoos, of coarse, but when we get back to the mountans, it'll all be back on us agin, so we need to plan accordingly. Not a thing is wasted, nor is unnecessary stuff accepted. We take only that which is required, the most important being that which allows us to survive, and second, the notes and specimens that Mr Jefersun desires so grately.

~ THERD PART ~
HOMEWARD BOUND

FINULLY its time fer us ta leev, an man are we ready! We been gatherin all are belongins onta horseback, an as much as we kin carry in the canoos, an gettin redy ta moov out. The Captans have decided ta give the Fort to the Clatsop Injuns, an we are settin out fer Home on March 23, 1806.

Captan Lewis surprized me by askin me ta say a few werds of thanks afer we set out fer the return trip home. I took off my hat an bowed my hed, an so did all the rest of the Core, even them wut ain't Believerz, an I sed, "Grate God of the Universe, jest like You brought them Children of Izral out of bondage in Egypt an led them to the Promised Land, so to Ya brought us heer ~ are Promised Land. We cood have rotted frum within by sickness, froze ta death or starved, but in Yer tender mercy You kept us hole, unharmed. We thank Ya, Lord, fer keepin us safe, despite all the obstacles between Home and heer. Now its time ta head back East, an we ask Yer hand ta guide an protect us all along the way. We thanks Ya fer all Ya dun fer us, an whut Ya has in store fer us on are return jerney. May we live out the rest of are dayz as a testimony to Yer surpassing Love. We pray all this in the Name of Yer only Sun, are Savyer, Amen." We then raised are heds, put are hats back on, loded areselves, the horses, an the canooz up, an moved out, heded fer Home, at last.

We made are way upstreem agin the currents of the Culumbia River, but we wuz healthy, an happy ta be on are way. The rowin wuz ruff, but we sang fer joy as we pressed on Eastward at long last. Retracing are corse, the way seemed easier than it had been heddin West, cause we new ware weed been afer, so wile the werk wuz hard, we bent are backs to it and were soon far frum the Western shore of the Pasifik Oshun.

On the way back tward the Nez Purse Injuns, we been meetin up with sum otheruns ~ the Cathumet, Watula, an Wala Wala tribes. The cheef of the last bunch, Yelleppit, tole us we cood save arselves about 80 milez ifn we took a shortcut he had in mind. Mebbe this wuz the shortcut Old Toby had been thinkin about way back wen we wuz headin West. We jumpt at the chanse, an Cheef Yelleppit wuz rite. Now we got back to the Nez Purse, who is all very hapy to see us agin. We are gettin more horses frum them (at a much fairer cost than from the Clatsops), an weer stayin a spell with em to rest up sum. Along the way we turned up sum of the cashes of supplies that we had stashed earlier, an now we can carry em agin as we hed back East.

　　I gotta tell ya, its alwayz comicul lisenin to all them Injun tribes try to translat back an forth between usuns an themuns. Weed start out in English, then to Frenchy, then to Hidasu, then to Shoshony, an finuly to Nez Purse an back agin. Back an forth, back an forth. It took HOURS just ta say a little bit! An even then we aint totally sure we both understand wut all we wuz sayin. By the end of are visit tho, Captan Clark tole me that the Nez Purse wuz the most hospitabul an agreeabul of all the Injuns weed come acros on are travuls, an I agreed with him.
　　As the travels over the mountans, frum the trip Westwards, wuz still fresh in our minds, we wuz mitey careful as we wer headin back into em

goin Eastward—as careful as we had been comin out thisaways. The wether may have been sunny an warm along the coste, but up heer it never seems ta git warm at all, an the snow covers the mountans all yeer long. We ran into sum drifts that were as much as ten ta fifteen feet deep, so we had ta be extra careful ta skirt around them areas.

Onest we left the mountains, we wuz goin on up the Culumbia River until we come to a parting of the ways. The Captans had desided the Core shood split up an do more discuverin on our return trip. Captan Lewis an his boyz went Northeast on the Maris River, an Captan Clark an his men (wich includes me, York, Sakajuweea, Pomp, Sharbono an sum others) are goin Southeast on the Yellerstone River. The Captans have pland ta meet up agin on the Mizura River a cupula weeks frum now.

Tother day a bunch of us hunters wuz goin out to get fresh game, and I noticed Captan Clark bangin on a rock down by the base of a mountan we named Pompeyz Piller, which we discuvered jest off the Yellerstone River.

"Watcher doin, Captan?" I asked him.

"I'm chiseling my name heer on this rock, ta mark the place where are Core of Discovery has passed, along with the date, soze other peeple will someday know that we were here, and when," he answered.

"That's a perdy good idee," I sed. "Mebbe this'll last fer all eternity, who knows?"

"Mebbe so, Danny. Mebbe so," he sed, thoughtfully.

Captan Lewisez' bunch had a very dangerus scrape with sum Blackfeet Injuns an mostly got out of it ok. But not afer they stabbed one of the Injuns, who had been trying ta steal their guns an horses! It wuz the first time in all are travels that we actshuly killed a Injun. Twuz a sad thing, too. It may have had a lot ta do with Captan Lewis's atitude ~ his depreshun. Mebee he took the Injun acts toward his partee too seriously, an his dark mood got the better of him. He may have lost all control. Anyhows, the Lewis party got away safe an sound, wich was a blessing.

A ways further on, after they got away from the red men, wile Captan Lewis an his bunch were comin to meet up with the rest of us, a sorta funny thing happened ~ well, funny to us, but certainly not to Captan Lewis! Wile a cuple of them wuz out huntin, one of the fellas who cant see so awful good shot the Captan in the butt by aksident.
As soon as he figgered out wut he had done, he tole the Captan that he wuz terribl, terribl sorry. It must have taken a lot fer him ta say it, but the Captan jest tole him that accidents happen. Captan Lewis dint think it was funny at all tho. He had ta be carried fer a long, long spell either in the canooz or on horseback

(layin forward on his belly) an eventshully had to limp fer quite a ways. It weren't long after that afer the two groups of the Core met up with one another agin, an we wuz all excited ta be reunited.

It's wonderful ta finally be leavin the Rockees behind us, let me tell you! Jest the same, it's mighty fine ta look back West at them an realize that we actually made it the hole way thru em without losin a soul! Now that the Core is come together agin, its smooth sailin down the Mizura, with the curent quikly takin us downstreem. It had taken us about 1 ☐ years ta get all the way out West, but its only takin us around 6 munths or less ta get back to St Loois! Kin you believe it? The closer we gets ta Home, the more folks weer meetin up with. At first there were jest a few stragglers headin back toward wear wee jest come frum, but gradually more an more folks show up. Sum of em are headin West their own selves, ta git land or ta hunt or trap or trade. It shure is good ta see sumbudee new fer a change, espeshuly folks with Wite skin, an not Injuns all the time! An the closer we git, the bigger the Welcome weer gettin, too. A lot of fokes figerd we reely had died out there in the Wildrnes a long, long time ago. Most everbody hadnt heerd frum us in so many munths an years that they thot we wuz goners fer sure. But lo an behold, heer we come, sailin down the Mizura River, just like weed poled up it so many munths afer. In there excitement ta see us, they been freely givin us gifts of tobakee and spirits and various foods that we hadn't seen frum "civilizashun" in many a live long day! Its so gud to be neerly Home at last.

Its been a munth now since Captan Lewis was shot an Captan Clark reports that his wounds are healed nicely. He's back to gettin around freely now, an can even run much like he did afer he was hurt. Another thing ta report is that the skeeters has been as bad as they ever wuz on are trip. It was nice ta have a break frum em wen the wether was cold an bitter, but the spring thru fall munths bring em back out in clouds of misery fer us an Captan Lewis' dog, Seaman, an the horses too. That's jest the way life is, I guess, unfortunately.

I bin struck down with Disinterree fer almost 2 weeks now. I feel weak as a babe, an kin hardly hold myself together long enuf ta dash off ta the latrine. I been mizerable sick, with teeth-chattering chills an skorchin hot fevers. Sum of the others wuz down with it too, so weev been laid up fer a short time, wile we heal. I'm feelin sum better now, but still tired an weak. The least thing on my mind had been ritin in my Jernal.

A few days after the Core had started out agin, jest as weer gettin neerly back to Saint Looee, Johnee Colter come up ta me an sed, "I'm fixin ta take my back pay an buy supplies. Then I'm gonna hed back West agin, neer the Yellerstone River that we an Captan Clark explored. You wanna come with me?" Johnee asked.

We had herd rumers about crazy things to be seen in them parts. Mebbe we cood even find sum of Prezident Jeffersun's woolee elephunts fer him. Nobody knows wuts out there.

    I had ta think on it a bit, but altho the idee wuz a bit temptin, I wuz reely tired of travelin. "No Johnee, thanks fer askin, but I'm plum wore out, ta tell ya the truth. I gotta rest up fer a spell. Mebbe I'll head back West some time later, but not fer now. You go ahead though. Sounds like a good idee."

~ FORTY PART ~
PEECE AN QUIET

Now that weer finally back, theyz havin a big todoo round heer. It started around Saint Looee, where the rest of the Core had begun their jurney, an festivutees went on fer dayz. Captan Clark tole me its September 23, 1806 an weer in Saint Looee about three years after the Core had started its grand trek. Therez parteez an paradz an danses; I went to a cuple, even tho I caint danse. Its kinda fun, I ges, but I dont know wut all the big fus is about. We did jest wut we set outta do, fer the most part, even tho we dint find the Northwest Passaj everbodee wuz hopin weed come acros (speshuly the Prezident). Sum of the men might even meet Prezident Jefersun sumday soon over in Virginnee (but thats not fer me). Most of the fellas are reely enjoying bein back amungst all theez peeple, an I'm glad fer em, but fer me, it almost seemz like a let~down feelin. I noticed that Captan Lewis seemz ta be feelin the same way. He looks all happy an content on the outside, but underneeth therez that look of sadness in his eyes ~ a lot like wile we was gettin redy ta hed east agin, out on the coste. I wunder wut'll happen ta him. Fer myself, I'll jest be glad ta let things settle down. I jest wanna find me a place I kin call Home, an let the outside world take care of itself.

At last the shindigs have died down sum, weer all kinda goin are seperut ways, litl by litl. It's kinda sad ta watch us all go off in diferent directions. Who noz if we'll ever see each other agin? We who wuz all jest like bruthers are watchin as bit by bit the Core gits smaller an smaller. Its like one big family that grows up an moves away, ta find an grow there own families. That's probably what I'll do to when the time comes, an it seemz ta be comin soon.

Back heer amongst civilizashun there are two things wut drives me neerly madd. The firstun is that a body caint get a minutes peese an quiet ta themselves! Its noiz, noiz, noiz all day an all nite. Out in the wild, a body kin heer hisself think, an lissen to the birds, animuls, an even the wind russlin in the treez. The uther thing I kin hardlee stand, sinse I aint used to it no more, is all them lites at nite. In Godz great outdores, ya kin see the stars in all there gloree! The bugs wut fly around at nite and the other critters like owlz an bats wut fly thru the dark sky is vizibul against the moon an stars up abuv. Heerabouts there are lites blazin frum dusk ta dawn an the sky is neerly hid frum view completely. It'll take a long time fer me ta git back into the "civilized" way of life agin; persunulee, I kin do without it jest fine.

The Core has dispersed, an I kinda dowt peepl will even remembr us in the yeers ta come. But who knows? Wut we dun wuz perty Speshul come ta think on it ~ wut we dun had nevr bin dun befor by Anybodee else, septin that feller up in Canada who werked fer that Fur Cumpanee ~ so mebee therez sumthin ta remember about the Core of Discovery in the Futur after all.

I gotta tell ya, Im sick to death of travelin an explorin. Allz I wanna do is settle me down

somewherez an farm an mebbe raise me a family, too. I think I'll head me back to the Ohia country, toward the north someplace wear there aint much biznus goin on. I hear tell that the area round Ft. Defiance aint bad ~ not too loaded down with peeple yet ~ an the farmland is wunderfulee rich an sweet an grate fer growin crops. I heered that sum of the Injuns are still fussin about who owns the land, an keep tryin ta kick us out, but I think therez not a lot of danger left anymore. I cood be wrong tho. There's a huge area thats mostly cuvered with shallow water an mud, but after all I bin thru, it'll be a lot different than wut I've seen over the past cuple of yeers. Besides, I cood stil hunt an fish an trap up there pert neer as much as I do out heer. Mebbe I'll try my hand back thataway. Theyz got a few towns started over by Fort Defiance an Fort Wayne. The people thereabouts call it the Grate Black Swamp, back Ohia way. I guess we'll jest haf ta see wut turns up. I dont know nobody back there, but then, I dint know nobody wen I joint up with Captans Lewis an Clark an their Core of Discovery neither. Reckon Ill find sum folks, an wen I duz, there'll be sum good woman I can hook up with ta start a family all my own. God only knows, but He's dun alright by me so far in this life, aint He? Yep, it'll be gud ta have a regular roof over my hed agin, an thats fer sure!

I mooved ta Fort Wayne, in the Indiana Teritory fer the first while since we got back from our Jurney West an back agin. Since then, I got my eye set on a piece of land in the northwest corner of the state of Ohia, an I'm fixin ta bild a cabin over there as soon as I'm able. Nother thing I been doin is goin over my notes frum the Jurney, an I begun rethinkin stuff thats gotta be sed.

    In the cuple of years since we came home to the States, I found me a right fetchin woman, an soon we got wed. Weez happy together, an she has incuraged me ta put this heer Jernal in order so others kin know wut I noz an mebbe see a peese a wut I saw. I hope I dont let em down.

    Fokes like Captan Lewis, Captan Clark, xprezident Adams an Mr Jefersun, are all reel smart an edjucated men. A fella like me dont seem ta need much more edjucashun than I gots, since I mostly hunt, fish, trap, an now farm. But wen I think on wut else I might be or do if I had more skoolin, who noz wut I cood do? Mebbe I cood even be Prezident myself sumday. I think thats wut Amerika's all about. We start out as yungins, noin nuthin, an a bit at a time we grow ~ both in age, in size, an in knowin things. An afer ya no it, yer Prezident! Aint that sumthin! But I am wut I am, an my wife Emma an I are as happy as a pare of chikadees. Fact is, we jest had us a baby boy, who has curly, reddish~brown hair. We named him William Meriwether Mueller. Sounds rite fittin, huh?

Im all settled into the next step in my life now, an as I think back on things, my only reel regret is that I dint take time ta rite

more detales down or spend more time describin the experiences that took place on our Jurney. It wasnt as though there hadnt been a lot ta rite about. There wuz always lots ta see an heer an smell an think on an talk ta one another about. A fella with more time on his hands cooda rote pages every day, probly. But ever single day was a busy and egzausting one. In kind of a summary: frum the time we got up in the morinin, we hedded down to the River fer the dayz werk. Everbody had a job an everbody did it. Everone wuz equal in that way. As a hunter/scout, much of the time I wuz on shore werkin with Captan Lewis. But sometimez we set out on are own. We had ta look out fer the needs of the Core, an their constant hunger was the same as are own. Wether on shore or with the botes, we all had hard werk ta do ever day. Ifn you wuz with the botes, ya had ta be reel careful not ta let the current get away with ya. If ya did, mistakes cood make us lose the werk of many hours worth of progress in jest a few minutes. All of us wuz strong, helthy men, but by the end of every day we wuz all plum wore out. Weed tie up the botes, make camp, eat our vittles, an soon we were sound asleep, unless we had skeduled guard duty that nite. Anyhows, ritin in a Jernal wasnt a priority. The Captans did most of that. So most of us left the majer piece of the recordin to themuns who knew the most an best.

A few yeers followin are return to St Loois, I heer tell that Captan Lewis has died. I dont know wut happened, but mebbe he gave in to them sad feelins he often had. God only noz.

So, fer anybudy who might someday read wut I been ritin about, this has been the Trew Tale of my Travelz out to the Pasifik Oshun with Captans Lewis an Clark, an their Core of Discovery. I reely hope that sum of this makes sense to you an if you kin even get a small idea of wut all I been thru, I've had a bit of success. I honestly pray that God will bless you all, an may He espeshully bless these United States of Amerika! That may sound like sum high an mighty thinkin, but I reely mean it. Good-bye to you all. D.M.

\>\>\>\>\>\>\> **CORPS OF DISCOVERY** <<<<<<<

Captains
Meriwether Lewis
William Clark

Sergeants
Charles Floyd
Patrick Gass
John Ordway
Nathaniel Pryor

Privates and
William Bratton
John Collins
John Colter
Pierre Cruzatte
Joseph Field
Reuben Field
Robert Frazer
George Gibson
Silas Goodrich
Hugh Hall
Thomas Proctor Howard
Francois LaBiche
Jean Baptiste LePage
Hugh McNeal
John Potts
George Shannon
John Shields
John B. Thompson
Peter M. Weiser
William Werner
Joseph Whitehouse
Alexander Hamilton Willard
Richard Windsor

Non-Military Members
Toussaint Charbonneau
Sacagawea
Jean Baptiste Charbonneau
Baptiste Deschamps
Pierre Dorion
George Drouillard
York, Captain Clark's slave

Non-Human Members
Seaman, the dog

{ Private Daniel Mueller }

RESEARCH SOURCES:

Ambrose, Stephen E., *Lewis & Clark: Voyage of Discovery.* Washington, D.C.: National Geographic Society; photographs by Sam Abell, 1998.

Ambrose, Stephen E., *Undaunted Courage: Meriwether Lewis, Thomas Jefferson, And the Opening of the American West.* NY: Simon & Schuster - Ambrose-Tubbs, Inc., 1996.

Burns, Ken, *Lewis & Clark: the journey of the Corps of Discovery.* 2 videodisks (240 mins.). Boston, MA: WETA –TV, produced by Dayton Duncan and Ken Burns; written by Dayton Duncan, 1997.

Duncan, Dayton & Ken Burns, *Lewis & Clark: The Journey of the Corps of Discovery, an illustrated history*, NY: Alfred A. Knopf, Inc., American Lives Film Project, Inc., 1997.

Eide, Ingvard Henry, ed., photographer, *American Odyssey: The Journey of Lewis & Clark.* Chicago, IL: McNally & Co., 1969.

Foley, William E., *Wilderness Journey: the Life of William Clark.* Columbia, MO: The Curators of the University of Missouri; University of Missouri Press, 2004.

Jones, Landon Y., ed., *The Essential Lewis and Clark.* Landon Y. Jones: Harper & Collins Publishers, 2000.

MacGregor, Carol L., ed. & annotated, *The Journals of Patrick Gass: Member of the Lewis & Clark Expedition*, Missoula, MT: Lynn MacGregor; Mountain Press Publishing Co., 1997.

Moulton, Gary E., ed., annotator, *The Lewis & Clark Journals: The Abridgement of the Definitive Nebraska Edition.* Lincoln & London, NB: The Board of Regents of the University of Nebraska, [incl. Map & Members of Corps of Discovery], 2003.

National Geographic Television & Films, *Lewis & Clark: A Great Journey West, 1 videodisk* (40 mins.). Washington, D.C.: Geographic Society, director, Bruce Niebaur; producers, Lisa Truitt & Jeff T. Miller; written by Mose Richards, 2002, 2004.

Quaife, Milo M., ed., *The Journals of Captain Meriwether Lewis and Sergeant John Ordway kept on the expedition of western exploration, 1803-1806.* Madison, WI: State Historical Society of Wisconsin, 1916.

Ronda, James P., *Finding The West: Explorations With Lewis & Clark.* Albuquerque, NM: The University of New Mexico Press, 2001.

Woodriger, Elin & Brandon Toporov, *Encyclopedia of the Lewis & Clark Expedition* NY: Woodridger & Brandon Toporov; maps c. 2004 – Facts on File, Inc., 2004.

ACKNOWLEDGEMENTS

First and foremost I wish to thank my precious wife, Rebecca, an author in her own right, for editing this most difficult text. I am extremely grateful to Stacy Lynn Andrews, a talented artist, who agreed to do the many sketches found in this book. God has gifted her so graciously! To those who have gone before, from Lewis & Clark and their Corps of Discovery, to all those who have researched and written about their exploits, I have been so excited by their many works. They have helped me tremendously in the writing of this historically accurate novel. I'm thankful Too for my eldest son, James' wise advise, as well as his computer savvy. In addition, I appreciate the Dog Ear Publishing Staff, which is producing this book for me, specifically Megan and Adrienne who answered all of my questions and guided us to the completion of the book. And above all else, I give praise and thanks to God, Who has given my the ability to write, with imagination and great joy.

Personal Addendum:

A number of years ago I was taking an interesting class in U.S. / Canada Geography instructed by Pete Wilhelm at Northwest State Community College, of Archbold, Ohio. Naturally, a term paper was required at the end of the semester. Here's where the excitement began: instead of turning in a "normal" assignment, I received permission to write a Journal as though I was a member of the Lewis & Clark expedition, aka "Daniel Mueller." That 12-page paper blossomed over the years into the book you now hold in your hands.

    I created "Danny" as a relatively uneducated hunter, trapper, and guide in his early twenties, who as he met up with the Corps of Discovery on their way westward, determined to write a Journal of his exploits. His writing was not spelled correctly, but by how words "sounded" to him, phonetically. While Danny himself is a fictional character, all of the other occurrences throughout the story are factual, making this an historical novel.

    I hope you found enjoyment in his view of events, even as you learned of the details that occurred during that 1803-1806 adventure into the wild unknown, west of the Mississippi River and into uncharted Indian territory.

David L. Miller

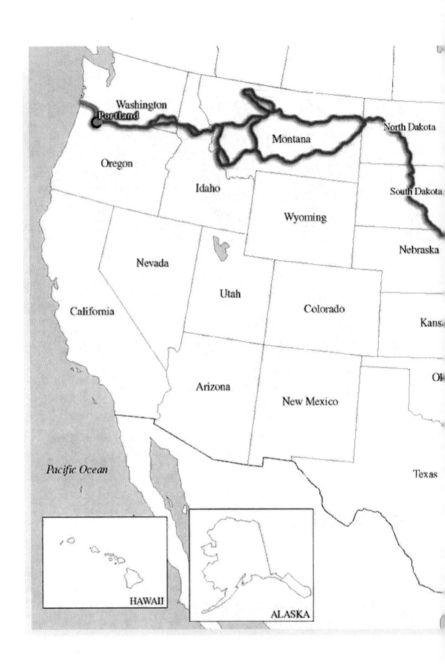

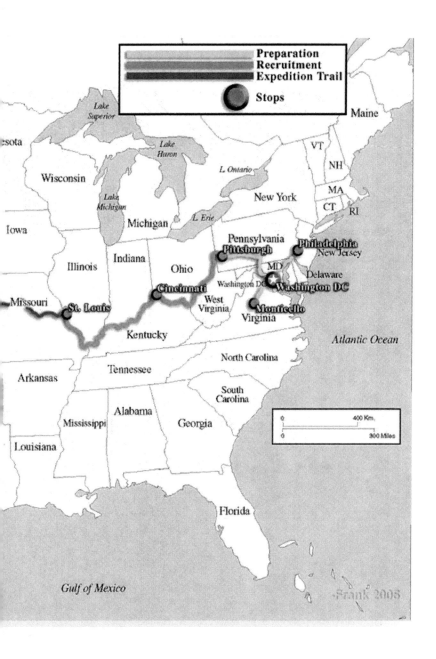

This is the first publication for
Mr. Miller
and
Miss Andrews.

 David Lynn Miller, a native of Archbold, Ohio, has loved American history since his elementary school days. This book is his way of sharing what it must have been like to be a part of the Lewis and Clark Expedition, through the eyes of his characterization, Daniel Mueller. David attended college at Eastern Mennonite in Virginia where he met his wife Rebecca Hutchins Miller. He is a graduate of Elim Bible Institute in Lima, New York, with a Bible major, and a double-minor in Ministry and Missions. He has also taken classes at Taylor University/ Ft. Wayne campus and is close to attaining an Historical Preservation Associates Degree from Northwest State Community College in Archbold, where he achieved Phi Theta Kappa status, the National Honor Society for two-year colleges. David and his wife live in rural Williams County, Ohio, have 4 grown children and 6 grandchildren. He can be reached at dlrlm15@gmail.com .

Born in Defiance, Ohio, Stacy Andrews was inspired from a young age by quiet moments alone with a pencil and paper. Art lessons helped Stacy fill her sketch books and she went on to explore art forms including, but not limited to, oil paint, pastels, metal-point, red chalk, and watercolors, her favorite being graphite. In 2012 eighteen-year-old Stacy received the Gold Key Award by the Alliance for Young

Artists and Writers. She is a second year student at Atelier Lack Studio Program of Fine Arts. With many illustrations, Stacy leads readers on a journey through "Daniel Mueller's" pioneer memoir, *A Travelerz Trew Tale*. After many hours of landscape study, Stacy's illustrations bring to life the untouched world of the old west. She enjoys the little delights of her own scenery, nestled in the city of Minneapolis, Minnesota. For more information about Stacy Andrews and her artistic talents, email her at andrest8@live.com or follow her on Facebook.

This is the first publication for both David and Stacy.

CPSIA information can be obtained at www.ICGtesting.com
Printed in the USA
LVOW11s0050010716
494797LV00002B/6/P